RUDOLPH
The Red-Nosed Reindeer
Shines Again

ADAPTED FROM THE STORY BY ROBERT L. MAY
ILLUSTRATED BY DARRELL BAKER

A GOLDEN BOOK • NEW YORK
Western Publishing Company, Inc., Racine, Wisconsin 53404

Copyright © 1982 by Robert L. May. All rights reserved. Published by arrangement with Follett Publishing Company, Chicago, Illinois. Printed in the U.S.A. by Western Publishing Company, Inc. No part of this book may be reproduced or copied in any form without written permission from the publisher. GOLDEN®, GOLDEN & DESIGN®, A LITTLE GOLDEN BOOK®, and A GOLDEN BOOK® are trademarks of Western Publishing Company, Inc. Library of Congress Catalog Card Number: 80-85028 ISBN 0-307-04601-X/ ISBN 0-307-60246-X (lib. bdg.)
K L M N O P Q R S T

RUDOLPH the Red-Nosed Reindeer was unhappy. Last Christmas he had been a hero. His shiny red nose had lit the way for Santa's sleigh. But since then the other reindeer had been jealous and unfriendly.

"Well now, Red Nose," said Dasher. "Let's see *you* carry this sack to the sled."

Rudolph tugged and pulled, but the sack was too heavy for him. Finally it burst open. The other reindeer laughed.

By the time Rudolph had put all the presents back in the sack, the others were playing on the snow-covered slopes.

At suppertime Rudolph sat off in a corner alone, eating his mince pie and feeling very sorry for himself.

Later, Santa and the other reindeer began to get ready for the big Christmas Eve journey. Rudolph watched from the window.

"No one likes me," he thought, wiping away a tear.

Then he noticed his reflection. "My nose doesn't even shine any more!" he said. "Santa certainly won't need me now. I might as well leave."

Rudolph wandered away toward the forest.
In the dark, six glowing eyes shone from behind the
trees. Three wolves were watching Rudolph. But Rudolph
didn't see them. He was too busy feeling sorry for himself.

Suddenly Rudolph stopped. He heard someone crying.

There, at the edge of the forest, he saw a family of very sad rabbits.

"Why are you crying?" he asked.

"Our two youngest babies are lost!" said Father Rabbit.

"The wolves are sure to get them!" wailed Mother Rabbit.

The rabbits looked so small and helpless that Rudolph felt big and brave and strong.

"Don't cry," he said. "I'll find your babies."

Rudolph charged into the forest. *Crash!* He banged into a tree trunk. He had forgotten that his nose didn't light up any more. But that didn't matter. He would find the baby rabbits somehow.

Rudolph stood still and tried to remember all his reindeer lessons.

He twitched his big ears—so he could hear better.

He wrinkled his nose—so he could sniff better.

Then he moved quietly through the woods, listening and sniffing.

Suddenly he heard a strange noise. And he sniffed a strange smell.

There, hiding beneath a bush, were the two baby rabbits, shivering with cold and fright.

"Don't be afraid," said Rudolph softly. "I've come to take you home. Jump onto my back and away we'll go!"

As he sped through the forest, Rudolph saw the three wolves.

He zigzagged through the trees, twisting this way and that. He ran so fast the wolves could not keep up with him.

Finally Rudolph got back to the edge of the forest.

How happy Mother and Father Rabbit were to see their babies! And how proud Rudolph felt!

"Please stay with us," said Father Rabbit. "We're going to have a wonderful Christmas party."

When he heard the word "Christmas," Rudolph remembered Santa.

"Thank you," he said to the rabbits, "but I have to go home. Santa may need me tonight. I know now that I can help, even without a shiny nose. Good-by, and merry Christmas to all!"

Rudolph started running. Faster and faster he went,
until he was flying through the dark sky. When he looked
down, he discovered that he could see the ground.

"Why, my nose is glowing again!" he cried. "I wonder if
the light came back because I stopped feeling sorry for myself."

Far below, Rudolph saw Santa and the reindeer.

"Oh dear," Santa was saying. "It's getting so foggy I can't see a thing. Where, oh where is Rudolph with his shiny red nose?"

The other reindeer hung their heads in shame. They knew why Rudolph wasn't there.

Just then a rosy glow lit up the snow. With a *zoom* and *whoosh*, Rudolph landed.

"Sorry I'm late," he said. "Some rabbits needed help. They had lost their babies."

"Did you find them?" asked Santa.

"Yes, I did," said Rudolph, and his nose glowed even redder with pride.

"Hurray for Rudolph!" shouted the reindeer.

"Now let's be on our way," said Santa.

"We're sorry we were so mean and jealous," said Dasher as Santa hitched him up behind Rudolph.

"That's all right," said Rudolph. "The important thing is that I stopped feeling sorry for myself."

Then they were off.

"Thank goodness for Rudolph and his bright, friendly light," said Santa. "Without him there would be no merry Christmas for children tonight!"

And off in their cozy den, the rabbits whispered,
"Thank goodness for Rudolph and his brave, kind heart.
Without him there would be no merry Christmas
for rabbits tonight."